Leaving Trauma Behind

Family Growing Pain
By:K.Moore
Book 2
Volume 1

Family Growing Pains

Leaving Trauma Behind, Volume 1

K.Moore

Published by Nakeia Davis, 2024.

Printed in the United States of America.

For more information, or to book an event, contact :

(relatablefictionwriting@gmail.com)

http://www.[1]relatablefictionwriting.com

Book design by (Nakeia Davis)

Cover design by Canva)

ISBN - Paperback:

ISBN - Hardcover :

First Edition: March 2024

---

1.   http://www.website.com

FAMILY GROWING PAINS

First edition. September 23, 2024.

ISBN: 979-8224020744

Written by K.Moore.

Also by K.Moore

Bonded By Love (Malcolm)
Bonded By Love (Malcolm)
Bonded By Love (Harmony's Story)
Bonded by Love (Christian's Story)
Bonded by Love (Janette&Ramona's Story)

Leaving Trauma Behind
Leaving Trauma Behind
Family Growing Pains
Turning a New Leaf
The Golden Years

The Byrd Song Diaries
The Byrd Song Diaries:Relationship Entryway
The Byrd Song Diraries: The Dating Games
The Byrd Song Diaries: The Marriage Act
The Byrd Song Diaries (Everyday People Skills)
The Byrd Song Diaries:That's not my problem

The Crash Out
The Crash Out:Teen Drama
The Crash Out: Teen and Adult Drama Continues

The Williams Family .....presents
A Letter to Trauma Victims
4 Seasons of Love
M.A.(Marriage Anonymous)
In the Line of Duty
A Father's Redemption
The Next Generation

Watch for more at urbanfictionwriting.com.

Table of Contents

To those who think there's no one out there for you and you'll be alone forever. There is someone out there for you just let God lead you to them.

These are our Family Growing Pains

Dedication

To all who are in blended families with drama, it will get better. Just keep praying like Zeek and Kahlani; it won't last too long.

1

Vacation Interrupted

AFTER THEIR ENGAGEMENT celebration concluded Zeek and Kahlani went back to the resort with their children. Then Janette returned 2 hours later to the resort with a list of everyday activities for the remainder of their trip. The next day the kids wanted to spend the day with Rosemarie and James. Ramona gave the concierge a list of relaxing activities for the newly engaged couple.

After having breakfast in bed the couple got dressed to go out for the day. As they entered the lobby , the front desk clerk stopped them saying they were going in the wrong direction. Then she asked: are you two the newly engaged couple? In unison they said "Yes we are" as Kahlani waved her ring at the receptionist. The clerk informed them of their couple's massage, facials, and mani/pedi before radioing for the spa's hostess to come get the couple.

For the next 3 days the couple enjoyed all the love shown by the islanders. The couple spent the next 4 days with the family touring the island of Hawaii together, with Independence Day coming up the couple wanted to experience everything around them. After the excitement of their engagement and tourist attractions Zeek and Kahlani were heading out with their children for the 4th of July. Janettehad already called Rosemarie saying they were on the way to her home. Just as they were about to walk out of their room, there was a knock at the door. I'm already in the kitchen. I'll get it; Janette shouted to the family. The knocking became louder just as she placed her hand on the doorknob. Upon opening the door Janette was shocked to find Malcolm's Mother Melody there. Melody was intoxicated,angry and looking extremely rough.

Before the door opened Melody started to change her mind about her actions on this day for fear of Zeeks' reaction. Roger had gotten into her head and turned her out in the streets and away from her dreams. At first she didn't want to be a mother but she wanted to be with Zeek. Her jealousy of seeing him happy with other women was the fuel that led Melody to this point. The Drugs and Alcohol were the match that made her feet come to this room today. Her son was practically an adult on this day, looking just like his handsome father everyday. It just made her heart hurt that Zeek moved on and didn't wait for her to come back to him.

2

Melody's Jealousy

"MELODY WHAT ARE YOU doing here, are you stalking my son?" Janette asked. "Yeah; I've been following his ass to make sure my son is safe." "Girl you should've been taking care of your son for the last 16 years with my son. Not lurking in the shadows stalking the man and trying to ruin his happiness. Well clearly you're drunk so go back to wherever you were staying and sleep it off. We'll meet up and talk tomorrow."

Before she could turn to leave, Zeek came around the corner surprised. "Melody what are you doing here? Why do you look like a miniature version of Slenderman? What have you done to yourself?" Clearly Zeek is upset by this unexpected visit. "Wait til he finds out about Destiny trying to snatch Harmony at the park." Melody then turned to go back to her room on the first floor. In her room alone she picked up the phone and placed a call. On the other end was the voice of Roger Williams asking what she found out. "He's engaged to marry some chick named Kahlani and they're here to visit her family. She's got to go, she's too pretty to be around my son." "Don't worry let me know when they get home, I'll be in Richfield to deal with her."

"You sound like you have history with her or something." "I certainly do" and hope she'll be up for a reminder of our past encounters. Did you do the same things to her that you did to me when I was with your son? Your situation is different from what I had with her and secondly I hate my son and that trash bag of a mother of his. I Don't know how she got out of my clutches when I had her so strung out that she should have been dead within a week.

Now I have to figure out how to get them out of the way so I can get to Kahlani. We have some unfinished business to attend to and we should have finished this after her father died. With a dreamy look in his eyes Roger said that there is no woman on the earth that can make a man's heart race like Kahlani. This made Melody very unhappy and she had to voice it to Roger. She stared at him like he was crazy on the facetime call. How can you go around making all these women feel like they're the best thing you've ever seen but worship only 1 woman that doesn't want you.

With a menacing glare Roger turned to Melody wanting to slap her so hard that she saw stars. Telling her: you just stick to the plan and do as I say, don't compare yourself to my history with her. She'll be a good girl for me once I get her alone and she gives me a child that looks just like her. Melody rolled her eyes mumbling to herself: I know and God knows that girl will never have a child with your old behind. Roger heard every word she said and didn't like it one bit. He spoke through gritted teeth: didn't I just tell you not to compare yourself to her just worry about what you are here to do.

3

Plan Goes Wrong

AFTER 3 WEEKS IN HAWAII the family was getting ready to head home. Once everyone was packed and headed to the airport, Zeek asked the driver to stop by Rosemarie and James's house for a moment, after saying their goodbyes it was finally time to go. But Ramona chose to stay with James and Rosemarie.

Once the plane landed back in Tennessee the family of 5 dropped off Janette next door. Kahlani asked Zeek to take her back to her house to get more of her clothes to move in. On the drive to her house Khalani received a call from her neighbor that was alarming. There was a black MKz parked in front of her home. Just as they arrived Kahlani asked Zeek to pull up beside the MKz. To their surprise Roger and Melody were sitting in the vehicle sound asleep.

Zeek was irate by the sight of his baby mama and a man he hasn't seen since 1986 here sitting in front of his fiance's residence in 2017. Looking at 2 people he hadn't seen in what seemed like forever. Being the officer he is, Zeek circled the block and called into the station. The operator Sandra came on the line asking what is his emergency. He replied. "Can you run a check on a black Lincoln MKz plate number FTK 2469." "Sure" Sandra replied "give me a second if you don't mind waiting."

It's cool, Sandy. I can wait. I just circled the block and I'm watching the vehicle. Okay, the vehicle comes back to Roger E. Williams, is there anything else I can do for you Zeek? Yeah can you run a check on Melody Stanton for me? Two minutes later Sandys' voice came back on the line. Melody has minor charges for public intoxication and prostitution. Thanks for your help Sandy but, I'm going to need backup at 421 E. Market St. Both Roger and Melody are there now, I think they plan to hurt my fiance' if I leave. Perplexed, Sandy asked; why do you think they're going to harm her Zeek? Melody has been stalking me for 16 years and mysteriously showed up in Hawaii while I was on vacation. Roger is my father and the co-defendant in a child molestation case from 1989 involving my fiance'.

Zeek this is crazy I can't believe you're engaged to Kahlani Coleman. That has been a cold case since Marcus Colemans' death. I know it's crazy as hell but I need them picked up ASAP. Zeek replies. I have units enroute to you Zeek they're 10 minutes away. Those seemed to be the longest 10 minutes of Zeek's life in that car in front of Kahlani's house. She leaned over the center console telling Zeek that once again she didn't feel safe anywhere. How had the man who raped and molested her 30 years ago found her again. Zeek held her hand and told her: you're always safe with me around baby, there's no need to fear.

No one has ever made Kahlani feel that she could trust them with her life. But this man sitting in the driver's seat was changing her heart with his words and deeds. Glancing in the back seat to see the faces of 3 innocent souls that she's grown to Love. All Kahlani could do was trust her knight in shining armor to protect her.

4

The past shows up again

Within those 10 minutes two units pulled up in front of Rogers' vehicle. Officer Meechum approached the drivers' side of the car, while officer Lewis approached the passenger side. Once both suspects were in custody Lewis walked up to Zeek and whispered"You didn't hear it from me but Destiny has been looking for you". It won't surprise me if you call for a car to pick her up too.If she starts stalking me and plotting to kill my woman,I'll be calling the coroner, not a patrol car to get her. This hefer here is working with my dad to hurt my lady and has got me extremely ticked off right now. I hear you man Lewis replied, let me get them down to booking I'll see you around Zeek. Yeah man let me get these 4 home and I'll meet you at the station. I have a lot of open-ended questions for both of them and I want answers quickly.

After getting Kahlani and his kids home Zeek made his way to the interrogation room at the station. Before he could get to the room Officer Lewis asked"who do you want to speak to first Zeek"? I want to speak to my baby mama first because she has 16 years of explaining to do. When he opened the door Melody was cuffed to the table and crying. With a stone-faced expression Zeek took a seat across from her and slammed the notepad of questions on the table.

Before Melody could react Zeek started his line of questioning glancing down at the notepad. 1)Why have you been stalking me instead of ringing the doorbell to see our son? 2)Why are you doing business with my father? 3)Why have you lost so much weight? 4)What went so wrong in life that led you to being a heavy drinker?

5)Why the hell are you a prostitute,when you left our son on my doorstep claiming you were going to be a lawyer?

With her head down Melody tearfully stated the answers to Zeeks' questions. First of all I didn't know Roger was your father Zeek I'm being honest. Everybody on the streets refer to him as E. That's all I know him as. Zeek interjected"how could you not know he's my father woman, me and Malcolm look just like him". Melody continued, He said he wanted to get closer to you and Malcolm so I started watching you. Then I got jealous when I saw you with Destiny and that other girl. That's what led to me drinking a lot and caused my weight loss/ appearance. Roger noticed I'd do anything he said when I was intoxicated and that's how I got into trickin. When I told him what Kahlani looked like and how much I hated her, he told me to follow you guys to Hawaii.The reason I knocked on your door is because I didn't like the fact that she had the man I wanted to spend my life with. When we got picked up we were planning out how we were going to kill her. With this information Zeek looked at her saying" I've moved on and you need to do the same" then left the room.

Now it's time to talk to Roger regarding his actions over the years. Upon entering the room Roger looked up at Zeek with a sly smile then replied" would you look at this here, my son is a member of law enforcement". In no mood for pleasantries said"cut the crap Roger,I got questions and you have answers" let's get to it. 1) Where have you been all these years? 2) Why are you out here abusing innocent women? 3) What do you stand to gain from controlling others? 4)Lastly: why were you sitting in front of my fiance's house?

Roger proceeded to answer with a smile on his face. Son I 've always been around I was just waiting for that old hag that raised you to get out the way. Then your mother came back into the picture and so did the cops. So I sat in the shadows to figure out a new plan. As you can see it's easy to control these broads with promises, drugs etc. I stand to gain any and everything I want from them and that's the way I like it. As for sweet Kahlani, we have a history that I want to revisit. In complete disbelief of what his father was saying Zeek stood from his seat. Before walking out Zeek turned to Roger and replied"You're never getting out and I'll make sure of it".

Then he walked out heading home to his family unable to understand his father's mental instability. What a narcissistic fool to think he can talk about Zeek's woman like a trophy he won 30 years ago. This was not sitting well with Zeek at all. But he couldn't let his family see his feelings written all over his face. So everyday he would play it off as soon as he walked into the house.

Ch 5: Quality Time

Two months later on Sept 11th Zeek and Kahlani were sitting on the porch enjoying the warm weather. Malcolm came outside looking a little down about something. Zeek noticed first and asked worried "what's on your mind son"? Malcolm, seeming uneasy, replied: it kinda has to do with both of you guys. With concern Kahlani motioned for him to come have a seat and open his heart to them. 1) How are you dealing with what my mom and granddad tried to do? 2)When are we going to start planning the wedding?3) It's time to start picking out a college before graduation and I'm undecided.

Kahlani reached over to take Malcolm's hand and reassuringly gave it a squeeze. Then she told Malcolm if he'd like she'd help him choose a college to attend. As for Melody and Roger I trust your dad will keep us safe from them. Zeek leaned back on the railing watching their interaction with admiration for the woman he was going to marry. Kahlani looked over her shoulder with a smile in Zeeks' direction before continuing. As for the wedding I was just about to talk with your dad about it when you came outside. And don't worry you and your siblings will be involved in the wedding.

Overjoyed, Malcolm hugged Kahlani and ran back into the house to tell his siblings the news. Then Kahlani turned around to find Zeek all smiles with his arms open wide to receive her, So she happily walked into his strong embrace without hesitation. Zeek looked down at her and asked:when do you want to have the wedding beautiful lady? Kahlani looked up at him and said with certainty " I want to have 2 weddings if that's alright with you".

Baby anything that makes you happy is alright with me. What do you mean 2 weddings baby we only got 1 marriage license to get married. She smiled up at him saying: we can have 2 weddings because I want a traditional Hawaiian wedding and a civil ceremony at the

Kingdom Hall. That's where Mrs. Johnson raised me and I want to pay my respects to her. After hearing his lady's request Zeek got down on one knee again saying:I'll marry you anywhere as many times as you like.

After dinner while washing dishes Janette asked Kahlani had she picked out a wedding date? Well the first wedding will be on May 30, 2018 and the second wedding will be July 4, 2018 in Hawaii. We are having 2 weddings. Janette shouted excitedly in the middle of the kitchen. Then the kids came into the kitchen overjoyed by the news.Everyone was ready to start planning the wedding except Kahlani who was still letting it set in. I'm going to be someone's wife was on repeat in her head the whole time she was in that kitchen. Then she looked at Janette and said: I'm going to need a lot of help with these weddings. And that's what you've got me and your mother for baby. Everything will be fine. This was a sight that made Zeek a happy man, little did he know just how extra Janette was going to be in the preparation for this wedding.

Ch 6: Time to plan the wedding

By Thanksgiving Kahlani was tired of planning the wedding thanks to her future mother-in-law. Janette was acting more like she was the bride than Kahlani. The only good part about this wedding was that Ramona and her grandparents had the arrangements under control in Hawaii. When they got to the dress shop Janette face-timed Ramona to get her input on choosing a dress for both weddings. Then when we get to the caterer to try the food Janette is trying to flirt with the chef. How much sense does it make that she's trying to get a date while I'm trying to choose the food for "MY" wedding not hers. Then she went behind my back and fired my decorator saying that my decorations looked like Cindy Lauper in her"Girls just wanna have fun" video. Next, Janette asked for my money back from the florist, because she didn't like the centerpieces And lastly:Janette returned Harmonys' bridesmaid dress behind my back because she didn't like it.I'm a christian but somebody needs to stop Janette before I lose my religion over this wedding.

When Zeek got home Kahlani sat him down to figure out what to do about his mom. She replied, Handsome I love your mom but she's making our wedding all about her and not about me. He looked at his lady with compassion and said: Beautiful I'm headed next door to speak to her now and everything will be fine I promise you that much. Upon entering his mothers' home Zeek found her in the living room watching t.v. He sat next to her and proceeded to explain Kahlani's concerns. Ma, you need to let my bride have what makes her happy if she needs your advice then help her. Don't forget I'm marrying Kahlani. I'm not marrying you, please stop taking control of "MY"wedding.

Janette wasn't expecting her son to put her in her place like that. Maybe it was time for her to change her approach to interacting with her daughter-in-law. Janette sent a text to Kahlani asking if they could meet up the next day for lunch. Kahlani agreed and showed the conversation to Zeek before going to bed for the night. The next day the ladies met for lunch and Janette apologized for her actions regarding wedding preparations.

Ch 7: Change of plans

On Zeeks' 34th birthday Jan 1, 2018 Kahlani wasn't feeling well so she went to the E.R. After 2 hours of waiting Kahlani was called to the back by the nurse. At the end of her exam the nurse gave Kahlani a can of ginger ale to settle her stomach. Then the doctor came back into the room with Kahlani's test results. With a smile, doctor Swanson replied: Congratulations Ms. Coleman, you're 4 weeks pregnant.

Overwhelmed with emotion, Kahlani hugged both the doctor and nurse Jenny for the news. All the way home she tried to figure out how to tell everyone the great news. The first person to greet her was Christian asking worriedly; where have you been?I went to the doctor, I didn't feel good this morning, Kahlani replied. With fear in his eyes Christian asked are you Ok Lani? Yes, I'm better but I do have some news to share with everyone after dinner.Throughout dinner Christian tried his best to get the news out of Kahlani with no results. As soon as dinner was over Zeek turned to Kahlani and said" It is my birthday, where is my present beautiful"? Filled with excitement, Kahlani handed Zeek the envelope with her test results. Zeek opened it and read the results smiling with glee. Then he turned to Janette and the kids and shouted" We're having a baby".

This is the best news this family could ever receive other than the wedding itself. Now here comes Janette wanting to plan the baby shower. Zeek had to check her again and gain some understanding with his mom. You never got this excited about my other children. Why are you so hyped about this baby coming? Son it's because she's not standing there saying she doesn't want your child. Hearing this made

Zeek's heart glad and he leaned over to hug his mother . And I'm glad she still wants to marry you after dealing with all my antics. Zeek nodded and laughed saying: I'm glad to know that too.

Ch 8: New Edition Arriving

Now since we're having a baby the wedding will have to be postponed for another year. With the baby expected to come in October Kahlani moved the wedding to May 30, 2019. That way their bundle of joy will be 8 months old and a part of the wedding. Kahlani face-timed her mom and grandparents to share the great news but told them she didn't know the sex of the baby yet.

On February 14, 2018 Zeek decided to give his fiance a Baby Shower fit for not just any queen but his queen. This made Kahlani so overwhelmed with joy to see all her friends, especially Cora Fields and Regina Maxwell. Since they didn't know the gender of the baby Zeek asked everyone to bring neutral colored gifts. The party was a great distraction for Kahlani from the stress of planning the wedding and finding out about the baby. Close to the end of the party an uninvited guest appeared in the form of baby mama number 2 Destiny Richardson "Harmony's mother".

In a fit of rage Destiny marched over to Kahlani and punched her directly in the chest, folding the mother-to-be into the fetal position. As Cora and Regina ran over to attend to Kahlani Zeek grabbed Destiny by the shoulders slamming her against the wall and roared "how the hell were you able to get into this private party Destiny"? Destiny replied in a shaky voice " I asked the doorman if I could use the bathroom, then I followed the partygoers in here". Destinys' answer infuriated Zeek so much at this point,but his main concern was his fiance and baby. Next he looked down at Destiny with a menacing glare stating "Get out of here now and if she loses my baby because of you, I'll have you put away for murder".

Knowing the type of man Zeek is Destiny is willing to try calling his bluff on this one. Just like Melody, Destiny continued to stalk Zeek from afar with jealousy in her heart. On June 22, 2018 Zeek and Kahlani joined the rest of the family to see Malcolm graduate from High School. Before heading home Kahlani asked Malcolm if he wanted to go visit his mother or grandfather. Malcolm looked Kahlani in the eye and spoke from the heart saying "She treated me like a burden and now she wants to help my grandfather take away the only mother figure I've ever had". I have no respect for her and don't want to see her.

Three months later on September 2, 2018 Kahlani and Zeek welcomed a baby girl they named Camille Angelique Williams.

The little princess was just as beautiful as her big sister and mother. After being showered with so much love Camille was taken to the nursery. Zeek and Harmony made bets on who would get to give Camille a bath. The nurses even found the family to be so cute and loving with the little princess. When it was time for Camille's feeding she was missing from the nursery.

Ch 9: Kidnapping

When the nurse informed the family of the missing baby Zeek sprung into action. Leaving the room he took the stairs from the 5th floor to the first. Just as he got to the front desk he saw a woman with a baby running out the door. Giving chase Zeek caught up with the woman in the parking lot. Circling around her he stopped her asking if she needed help. When she turned around and glanced at the man in front of her. When she locked eyes with Zeek shear panic appeared on her face. With contempt in his eyes Zeek demanded that Destiny give back the baby. When Zeek reached for the baby Destiny bolted for her waiting car.

Zeek gave chase in his car while Kahlani and the kids were in tears full of worry over baby Camille. Zeek called the station for back up as he followed Destiny through the streets of Richfield. He informed dispatch that he was in pursuit of a Red Dodge Caliber plate number MTB 6143. Sandra took the information and let Zeek know units were enroute. Then he let Sandra know that there was a newborn baby in the vehicle which belonged to him. Zeek never knew fear until that moment thinking of Camille.

To his surprise Destiny drove straight to Zeeks' home and parked in the driveway. Zeek let the dispatch know that the suspect was at his house. Within 5 minutes a unit came around the corner blocking Destiny in while Zeek was parked behind her. Once the Officer got Destiny out of the vehicle Zeek opened the backdoor to check on Camille. The baby was wailing at the top of her lungs.

Hey, pretty girl daddy got you don't cry. Then Camille looked up at her daddy and Cooed. The next thing he knew the unit officer asked if he wanted to press charges against Destiny. Without hesitation Zeek looked at the officer saying: on behalf of my fiance' the answer is yes, but I have some questions for her when I get to the station. Then Zeek drove back to the hospital where he handed Camille over to Kahlani and left out the door.

Ch 10: Questions and Answers

Once again Zeek was questioning someone about interfering with his life. And here he was with his list of questions for another suspect. And again it's another jealous baby mama ticking him off about his family. When she saw the rage in his eyes Destiny knew Zeek wasn't going to be going easy on her. As he sat at the table Destiny was trembling with fear of what Zeek was about to say.

Here we go again question 1) Why were you at the hospital? 2) Why did you snatch my daughter from the nursery? 3) Have you been following me this whole time? 4) If so, how long have you been tailing me Destiny? She just sat there not saying a word, Zeek roared "answer me woman slamming his hand against the table.

With tears in her eyes Destiny finally gave Zeek the answers he asked for. 1) I was at the hospital to see if the baby would look just like you and Harmony. 2) When I walked by the nursery and saw she looked just like you I took her. 3) Yes I've been keeping tabs on you along with Roger and Melody. 4) We've been following you since you graduated from the police academy.To say Zeek was speechless is an understatement at this point to say the least. To think he had children with 2 crazy women and didn't even know it. Zeek stood and went towards the door but stopped next to destiny to state clearly: I can't believe you would do this. There's no way of getting out of this in court.

Then he exited the room mentally and emotionally drained. Upon exiting the room Zeek's partner Rashad Lewis asked: what do you want to do with her. I'm pressing charges now that I know she's been working with Roger and Melody. They're trying to kill my fiance' and take my kids from me. Can you believe she just sat there and confessed everything to me.

Ch 11: Day of Reckoning

It was a chilly Dec 10, 2018 when Zeek and Kahlani entered the courtroom, this being the second time for Kahlani. This time Kahlani won't be the only one getting on the witness stand. All the reporters kept shouting questions at both of them. Charges ranging from kidnapping, stalking, attempted murder,and prostitution for Roger Wiliams and his 2 co-defendants Destiny Richardson and Melody Stanton.

After being sworn in everyone took their seats for the start of court. The prosecution called their first to the stand who happened to be Zeek. The prosecutor proceeded to ask Zeek about his childhood with Roger at home as a caretaker. Kahlani braced herself for the full story of Zeeks' trauma at the hands of Roger. Hopefully it isn't anything like what she endured. Zeek proceeded to give a detailed description of Roger and his associates during his childhood. It started when I was 2 every time I cried he'd yell at me demanding that I shut up. Then he'd beat my mother for trying to cater to me when I was hungry or had a potty accident. I'd stand in the doorway and watch him inject my mother with heroin every other day.

The days in between were some of the best days of my life with my mother, then she got tired and ran away leaving me with our neighbor Mrs. Wilson. When he got home and saw the house was empty,he went around the whole block looking for me. I had just gone to sleep when he started banging on the door yelling for Mrs. Wilson. I was hoping she wouldn't open that door but once the door opened I heard his feet coming and began to cry. He picked me up and walked out the door shoving Mrs. Wilson as he passed her. I wish everyday that I had the strength to get away from him that night.Taking a deep breath Zeek proceeded with his story saying, The next 3 days he got drunk and smoked nonstop, he wouldn't give me anything to eat and wouldn't allow any of the neighbors to feed me. I tried to feed myself but he walked in the kitchen, took the cereal and ate it while having one hand around my throat. I couldn't breathe and just knew I was about to die. All I wanted then was a mother, but I had no idea where she was. On the third day I kept begging that guy over there to give me something to eat and he laughed in my face. Then the sun was starting to go down when I looked out the window in my room and the doorbell rang.

I thought someone was finally coming to give me something to eat, then the door to my room opened to reveal Roger and 2 young women staring at me menacingly. Then he pushed me on the bed and proceeded to take my clothes off and say we're going to play before I can have any food. One of the women started touching my genitals while Roger instructed her to perform oral on me. I tried to get away but Roger hit me in the chest so hard I couldn't breath. Next he told the other woman to put her breast in my mouth but I wouldn't open my mouth so he told both of them to leave so we could talk. Once the door closed he began punching and kicking me saying that I was never going to be a man so I must be gay. Then he broke a leg off a chair and turned me over on my stomach and proceeded to insert the wood into my rectum. I guess when the neighbors heard me scream they called the police, then he removed it and tossed it to the side and walked out the room closing the door behind him.

There wasn't a dry eye in the courtroom after hearing Zeeks' story. Even Kahlani had her head in her hands in tears for her charming prince. The prosecutor cleared his throat and asked his next question 2) Mr. Williams, how do you know the co-defendant Melody Stanton? Zeek looked over at a teary eyed Melody and answered honestly, she is the mother of my son Malcolm. 3) How would you describe her as a parent or as a person in general? Zeek replied as a person she was fun to be around until she got pregnant. Then she changed and didn't want our son so she left him on my doorstep with a note and disappeared. What do you mean she changed exactly the prosecutor asked? The whole time we were together I made sure to use protection with her because I knew neither of us were ready to be parents. She was persistent about us being intimate with one another and one night we didn't think about the condoms until after the deed was done. She came to my house 2 weeks later saying she was pregnant and I was happy about it. I changed my work schedule and even skipped school some days to be at every doctor appointment but she wasn't happy. The day after Malcolm was born she left him on my doorstep with a note saying: she wasn't ready to be a parent and wanted to live her life so I let her be.

OK, then my last question is how do you know Destiny Richardson? Zeek took another breath and replied; she is my daughter Harmonys' mother.

The prosecutor took a step back and turned to the defense table saying your witness. The DA turned to Judge Anthony and said; the defense rests your honor. Judge Anthony asked the prosecutor if he had any more witnesses. He replied Yes Your Honor, I'd like to call Kahlani Coleman to the stand. Kahlani made her way to the witness stand passing Zeek. Stopping in the middle of the floor looking up at Zeek, looking for some form of acknowledgement from him. With a slight head nod she continued up to the witness stand. After being sworn in the prosecutor asked her the same questions he asked Zeek. So Kahlani told the story of how Roger was friends with her father and helped him violate her for a year. I was 3 the first time Roger came to my home to hang out with my father Marcus.

On Friday of the next week he came back and he stood next to my dad at my bedroom door staring at me in bed. I looked up asking my dad what was wrong and why was he not in bed with mom.. Then he and Roger came over to my bed and pulled the sheets off of me. My father then said he forgot to give me a gift for turning 3. At first I was excited about getting a gift from my dad until I got to the guest room and noticed Roger taking off his clothes. Then I saw my father taking off his clothes as well and they were both smiling at me in a sinister way. My father said for me to take off my pajamas but I refused and went back to my bed when Roger grabbed me. My body was thrown onto the couch and my clothes were ripped off by Roger and my father was smiling. I told them I was cold and wanted to go to bed. Roger took off his underwear telling my father he gets to go first.

I didn't understand what he meant by that so I looked to my father and he said; fine just hurry up so I can have a turn. They took turns for seemed like an eternity taking my innocence and this went on every Friday night for a year.

When I turned 4 my stomach didn't feel right at all, so I told my mom I needed to see a doctor. She took me to the E.R. When the doctor finally checked on me he had a surprised look on his face as he told my mom that I was pregnant. My mom was the most surprised by the news,as a 4 year old didn't understand what was being said. I asked what was wrong with my stomach and my mother told me I had a baby in my stomach. When we got home my dad and Roger were there in their underwear in the living room. Then the sirens started getting louder outside the house and both of them thought my mom called them on the way home.

Marcus ran over to my mom in the kitchen and began to beat her with the gun he had in his hand. Roger stood there aiming at the door waiting for the police to enter. I stood on the floor filled with fear of the sight before me as my mother pleaded with my father to understand that the hospital called the police, not her.

Next thing I knew the police kicked the door and I'm standing between the entire mess in tears. I looked at my mothers' bloody body unconscious on the kitchen floor. I could hear the officers asking me to go with them and my father telling me to go stand next to Roger, but

I wanted my mom instead. After I walked over to see the full scene of my mothers' body and pieces of her brain on the cabinets I snapped. I walked to the officer and took his service weapon then opened fire in the direction of Roger and Marcus. I still don't understand how Roger wasn't hit by any of the bullets I fired in his direction. To answer your other question I only know that Melody is Malcolm's mother and he wants nothing to do with her. As for Destiny, she tried to snatch Harmony at the park while I was there with Zeek's mom Janette. Then when Zeek told me she stole our daughter from the hospital out of jealousy that was enough for me to know about her.

Ch 12: The Final Verdict

The courtroom was silent again at the conclusion of Kahlani's testimony so she turned to the Judge and asked if she could step down. The judge looked over to the defense table and asked if there were any further questions for the witness.The DA once again said he had no questions for the witness and was resting his case. The judge told the jury they were allowed to deliberate the case. Then he turned and told Kahlani she could step down and she was very strong. Kahlani nodded with a slight smile before going back to her seat next to Zeek in the gallery. Then Judge Anthony announced that they would reconvene after a two hour lunch break to get the jurys' verdict in the case.

Zeek escorted kahlani to a cafe across the street from the courthouse for their two hour lunch break. While in the cafe they both called their mothers' to keep them updated as well as to check on the kids. Zeek took Kahlani by the hand and told her she did great in the courtroom . You did also and I'm sorry for what you endured back then Kahlani replied. Once their food arrived the two ate then Kahlani asked Zeek would be ok with just going to Hawaii and having just one wedding instead of the two she originally wanted. Zeek looked at her with sincerity in his eyes and told her again "Whatever makes you happy is all I want baby and if that makes you happy I'm all for it". In that moment Kahlani thanked Jehovah for bringing this man into her life then checked the time .

They still had 20 minutes left until returning to the courthouse so they sat quietly holding hands for 10 of those minutes. Then Zeek paid the bill and they headed back across the street to the courthouse to conclude the trial. Getting into the building the couple made their way to the 2nd floor into room 201 where they took their seats. After 3 minutes the room was filled with tons of people from news reporters to neighbors waiting to hear the verdict. Once the Jury filed in and Judge Anthony took his seat at the bench everyone waited for the verdict to be read aloud. Judge Anthony asked the jury Foreperson if they came up with a verdict and was told Yes then handed an envelope to the bailiff. Judge Anthony looked out into the gallery and spoke to the audience, mainly Zeek and Kahlani.

Before I read this verdict I'd like to say to the victims of these crimes how sorry I am that you weren't protected back when these crimes occurred. Please accept my sincere apology for the justice system failing you when you were younger. Your stories of trauma have hurt my heart and made me form my own verdict in this case but, it's not just my opinion that matters in this situation. As for you Ms. Stanton and Ms. Richardson, how could you call yourself a parent when you threw your children away and said you didn't even want them. And lastly, Mr. Williams, you know you're a pedofile and should have never been allowed around any children and you should have registered with the state when your son was taken from you.

Then Judge Anthony opened the envelope and read aloud, "We the jury in the above and titled action find the defendant Destiny Richardson ``Guilty" of kidnapping, conspiracy to commit murder and Stalking". The jury in the above and titled action find the defendant Melody Stanton ``Guilty" of Stalking and conspiracy to commit murder. We the jury in the above and titled action find the defendant Roger Williams "Guilty" of sexual assault of a minor under 13, domestic assault of Janette Jackson and drug trafficking . Next Judge Anthony handed down the sentences of each defendant starting with Destiny. Ms. Richardson due to the circumstances of this case and your actions leading up to this day I hereby sentence you to 25 years in state prison, if that newborn had died before her father got to her you'd be getting a Life sentence. Now Ms. Stanton due to your actions leading up to this day I hereby sentence you to 30 years with the possibility of parole in 15 years. Now Mr. Williams as for you I hereby sentence you to 99 years with no chance of parole for the crimes you've committed over the years.

Ch13: Choice of College

Now that the case is over Zeek and Kahlani headed home to hold their children and rest easy for the first time in their lives. Upon arriving at their home reporters were out front waiting to ask about the trial and the verdict. Exiting the car Zeek told the reporters "We're happy that the trial is finally over and our children will be safe" now if you don't mind giving my fiance some space to exit the vehicle. The reporters stepped back to give Kahlani room to exit, then asked her about the verdict. Apprehensive at first, Kahlani looked around at all the tape recorders and microphones in her face. Then she told them that the Guilty verdict was long overdue for all those involved. Just before going in the house a reporter asked one last question before we go. What's next for you two now that the case is closed? Zeek replied, "we're going to enjoy being parents" and Kahlani replied as well " we're going to have our wedding in Hawaii" flashing her ring for the camera.

Just as Zeek closed the door behind them the kids came down the stairs to greet them with hugs. Malcolm was holding baby Camille who was smiling up at her big brother and cooing in his direction. The sight just made Kahlani so happy she started to tear up at how much they adored their little sister. Then Camille started to wail loudly in distress and Harmony took her and noticed she was stinky. I'll change her you guys relax, Christian can you go get her bottle out of the warmer in the kitchen for me, Harmony replied. Then they were off leaving Zeek and Kahlani with Malcolm in the living room. Malcolm asked, since the case is over can we look at these College apps this weekend? Kahlani said, "sure I'd love to take a look at them with you" and Zeek replied" it's hard to believe you're 17 and about to be a College boy like I was at your age".

Malcolm smiled bashfully saying, dad chill it's not that serious but, what is serious is this wedding so when do we start preparing for it Ma? At the sound of him calling her Ma Kahlani smiled and said "we'll start prepping after we deal with those College apps OK". Malcolm headed back up stairs passing his 13 year old sister carrying a bin of laundry. Going to the end of the hall he found 9 year old Christian feeding their 3 month old baby sister looking so content in the rocking chair in the nursery. Then he went to his room to pull out the numerous College apps he had to choose from.

Just before calling everyone to the table for dinner Harmony took Kahlani to the side to tell her something important to her. Ma there's this boy at school I have a crush on and he just asked me to be his tutor for English Lit. Stunned, Kahlani asked what the name of the young man was and Harmony replied, Zachary Jiles. Kahlani nodded her head saying; Ok but, I'll be in these tutoring sessions and if you get stuck I can take over. That sounds good to me Ma thanks for agreeing to go with me,I'm so nervous and our first session is on Monday after school. Once Camille was changed, fed and sleeping in her bassinet in the living room everyone sat in the dining room for dinner.

The next day Saturday Dec 11, 2018 after breakfast Zeek left for work and everyone else went back to bed except Malcolm and Kahlani. It was time to look at these College apps once and for all. So what do we have to choose from Mal,Kahlani asked walking up to the table with a cup of Orange Juice. Well we have Tennessee State, Richfield Community, or go out of state to Virginia Tech maybe NC State. Kahlani then asked what major are you interested in Mal? Ma was thinking of going into Criminal Justice like dad,I asked dad when I was 3 and he said that was a great idea. Since you are still a minor I think you should start with the community college then in two years you can go to school out of state. So how about we start the Richfield Community app then apply to the other 3 after you get your associates.

Sounds like a plan ma you made this easy for me to decide what to do about school thanks. Your Welcome Mal I'm going back to bed before your sister wakes up again I'll see you later. Don't worry ma if she wakes up we'll take care of her you get some rest until dad comes home for lunch.Thanks Mal I'm so happy to see how much you guys love Camille I wish I was loved like that when I was young. We do love you Ma just as much as dad loves you Malcolm answered. I know I'm just saying when I was 3 months old the only person that loved me like that was my mom. Now you have a whole family that loves you very much.

Ch 14: Obsessed Crush

Back to work on Monday Dec 13, 2018 Kahlani walked into her classroom to get ready for the day. A knock on the door caught her attention and she turned around to find Harmony standing in the doorway. Hey, Ma just wanted to remind you about our tutoring session at 4. Thanks for the reminder baby girl I will see later now get to class, you know how I feel about tardiness. Yes Ma'am I'll see you later ma then Harmony gave Kahlani a hug and went on her way. By the end of the day Kahlani went to the library to meet Zachary for his tutoring session. Harmony sat across from him at the table with her books spread out between them.

Kahlani took a seat at the head of the table and introduced herself to Zachary and asked what they were going to work on? We're working on a Composition of The Great Gatsby for Mrs. Roberts class. So Zack let's start reading the first chapter then we'll analyze the story starting from there Harmony says. Kahlani just sat back and watched Harmony take control of the tutoring session. Maybe she'll become a teacher one day just like Kahlani and ask her for tips in the Classroom. After an hour in the library it was time to head home and Kahlani asked if he had a ride home. Zachary told her he was taking the bus home and Kahlani said she would take him home on their way so he wouldn't be waiting for the bus in the dark alone.

After 5 tutoring sessions it was finally over and Harmony was relieved that she didn't have to be uncomfortable in a confined space with her crush. Then after the tutoring Zack started hanging around everywhere she went at school and after school. Kahlani made it clear that he was not to be stalking Harmony due to her father being a cop. But Zack didn't take Kahlani seriously and continued to follow her around at school. Harmony began to not like being around him anymore so she asked him to leave her alone but he didn't take that well.

One afternoon after school Zack cornered Harmony in the library and he was angry about her not wanting to be around him. Harmony tried to explain to him that she just wanted space from him now that his tutoring was complete. Zack was so mad that he hit her in the side of the head with the back of his hand. Harmony was so scared because she had never been hit by anyone before. Even the librarian was afraid so she called Kahlani while watching from a distance. Kahlani and Zeek rushed over to the library just as Zack was about to attack Harmony again.

To everyone's surprise he was holding her hostage in the library and Zeek being in cop mode tried to negotiate with Zack. Zack turned around and saw Zeek pleading for his daughter's safety but Zack used Harmony as a shield between himself and the adults. Zeek called for backup to come to the school library for a hostage situation involving his daughter at Creedmoor Middle School. Kahlani tried to reason with Zack and get him to let Harmony go because she could see the swelling on the side of her face where Zack had hit her. Zack Yelled across the room " She's my girlfriend now nobody can have her but me".

Harmony was in tears staring at her parents wanting to get free, then more police came into the library. Zack wasn't interested in anything anyone had to say all he cared about was being with Harmony. Someone got in touch with his parents to come down to the school regarding the hostage situation. Once Zack saw his parents he told them Harmony was the best thing to ever come into his life. Zack's mom tried to explain to him that he's scaring her and she won't like you if you hurt her son. Just please let her go son this isn't the way to get the girl, his father said.

Ch 15: moving forward to the wedding

Zack's parents took him home and pleaded with Zeek not to press charges against their son. Zeek told them it's not up to him the person they need to be speaking to is Harmony since she was the victim. So the next week Mr and Mrs Jiles approached Harmony in the parking lot next to Kahlani's car. Mrs. Jiles asked Harmony if she wanted to press charges against Zack? Harmony looked at her with sorrowful eyes and replied, no I just want him to stay away from me forever. Then she walked on into the school and went to her homeroom class which was Math. Everyone wanted to ask if she was OK after her ordeal with Zack.

Then outside Kahlani looked at Zack's parents sadly and walked into the building for her first class which is History. Between dealing with Harmony's trauma and video chatting with Ramona about the wedding was wearing her out. By the time Zeek turned 35 it was the home stretch leading up to the wedding. Zeek wanted to make sure everyone in the family was in a great mood everyday. On Feb 14, 2019 Zeek took Kahlani out for a night of Karaoke to remind her of their first date. With 95 days until their Hawaiian wedding a date night was much needed.

Kahlani also tried to spend as much time with each of the children as possible, especially the girls. Kahlani went to spend a day with Malcolm but she could tell he wasn't happy regarding what happened to Harmony. Mal looked at her and replied, Ma I'm just so mad I want to hit him just how he hit my sister. I know Mal we're all upset about it but,no one is more upset than your sister. I was thinking that for the wedding you could be your dads' best man. How does that sound to you? I'd be honored to do that for you and dad Malcolm answered with glee. That reaction made Kahlani extremely happy to know he was as happy about the wedding as she was.

Next it was time to talk with Harmony and make sure she was mentally alright. So how are you doing since the situation Harmony? She took a deep breath and replied,I don't know if I'll ever be able to trust a man in the future after that Harmony answered. I have a question for you Harmony, How would you like to be a Junior Bridesmaid in the wedding? Harmony lit up instantly at the mention of the wedding and her role in it. You do know you're going to have to pull your sister in her wagon since she's the flower girl.

Lastly, Kahlani took Christian to the park and to the trampoline park to talk about the wedding. So baby boy why have you been so quiet lately? Ma I'm worried about Harmony a lot Christian responded. Harmony will be alright all she needs is some love and I you have a lot of that right. I sure do ma and I have a lot of love for you and camille too. Kahlani gave him a sheepish smile and a hug saying, Thank You for being a great young man for your family.For the rest of the month everybody looked through wedding magazines with Kahlani and gave their opinion on everything. By March 19th it was time for Kahlani, Harmony, Camille, Cora, Regina and Janette to get fitted for their dresses. At the dress shop Harmony and Cora tried on their bridesmaid dresses first, which were A Line flowy flower print floor length gowns. Then Regina tried on her gown which was an asymmetrical cut with the same flower print as the bridesmaid dresses. Janette was next to try on her dress and here goes the show. Janette came out of the dressing room complaining that she can't get a man dressed like she's 94 when she's only 58. So Kahlani asked the dressmaker to turn the fuschia dress into a corset jumpsuit with a matching jacket.

Now it was time to see Camilles' flower girl dress and our little princess was simply devine in her white ball gown with removable skirt.

Lastly, Kahlani came out in her Ivory Mermaid gown with a satin train. Everybody was amazed by how beautiful she looked even little Camille was clapping when her mommy came out. Then Kahlani tried on her floral print cocktail dress for the reception. Once all the Vera Wang dresses were taken care of the ladies head home for the day.

The next day Kahlani took Harmony and Camille with her to meet with the caterer to sample the food. After the show Janette put on the last time Kahlani was not going to listen to her flirt with the chef again. Within an hour the menu for the reception dinner at the Kingdom Hall was ready. Kahlani made sure to have things everyone liked from Waffle Fries and Burgers for the groom, shrimp cocktail for Janette, mashed potatoes for the kids and Kahlanis' favorite veggie broccoli with cheese oh let's not forget the chicken.

Ch 16: Mens day with the boys

Aweek later Zeek took Malcolm,Christian,Officer Richards and his partner Officer Lewis to get fitted for their suits. Zeek beamed with pride seeing his two sons look so handsome in their Tom Ford suits. Then Richards and Lewis tried on their suits and there were some issues with the pants and jackets. The sleeves on Richard's jacket were 4 inches too short and Lewis' pants were 2 inches too short. Last but not least Zeek tried on his suit and that man was a sight to see for every woman walking past the tailor.

These 5 black men were stopping traffic as they exited the tailors' to go get lunch. Once they arrived at World Tavern for lunch heads were still turning in their direction. Even while they were eating, women would knock on the window by their table to flirt with them. Both Zeek and Malcolm shook their heads at all the attention they were receiving just trying to eat a meal. Malcolm was on his phone texting Kahlani about everything that happened that day. While Lewis and Richards were enjoying the attention they were getting the whole day. Zeek asked Christian who he was in such a deep conversation with on his phone. Malcolm looked over and laughed saying " He over here telling Ma every detail of the day and she is laughing at us".

Zeek smiled and pulled out his phone and placed a call to his bride to be who answered on the third ring after telling Christian she had to go. When the call connected Zeek put the call on speaker asking her " why are you laughing at our distress beautiful"? Kahlani laughed again saying "I'm not laughing at you, I'm laughing at how Christian described the women flirting with you". Zeek glanced across the table at his 9 year old who was still typing her another message and asked what did he say? Just then Kahlani let out a laugh that came from her gut, then Harmony could be heard laughing as well. Kahlani said: Zeek look out the window to see what we're laughing at.

There outside the restaurant was a middle aged woman with a sign saying "Are you looking for a sugar mama cause I got lots of sugar for ya". Everyone at the table was laughing hysterically except for Christian who was typing his opinion of these women to Kahlani. This was the best laugh any of them had in a very long time and around such good energy. Richards turned to Christian and replied: little man you do realize you're going to have women act like this towards you when you get older, right. Christian looked up at him and responded: I'm going to ask Ma to home school me from now on cause I don't have the sanity for this much attention. They shared one more laugh then it was time to head home for the night.

Ch 17: A month until the wedding

With a month left the couple along with Janette and their children met with the elders at the Kingdom Hall. Kahlani explained that she wanted to pay her respects to Mrs. Johnson by having a wedding there on June 25. All those who knew Mrs. Johnson were more than happy to give their time to see Kahlani get married. Most of them had helped Mrs. Johnson raise Kahlani in the Hall. Pleased with the meeting Zeek and Kahlani went home to pack for their trip to Hawaii for their destination wedding.

Entering the house they could see Malcolm had sat his suitcase by the front door and was helping Christian pack. Harmony was finishing up her packing with the help of Janette while Camille was sleeping. Then Janette went next door to her home to pack her bags as well for the trip. While packing she called Ramona to talk about what else needed to be done for the wedding. Ramona informed her that everything was under control and they had to show up and enjoy themselves. With the conclusion of the call Janette went back to her kitchen to get a meal. Then it was time for bed but, first she had to call her son and say goodnight.

The following two weeks were pure chaos to say the least with getting the suits and dresses shipped on time.The kids going to school to finish off their assignments before spring break. By May 26th it was time to get on the plane and head to the big island for the best day ever. In the airport there was a 1 hour delay until their flight was set to leave and the kids were cranky except Camille. With 30 minutes until boarding all the boys went for one last bathroom run followed by the girls. Once on the plane comfortably all the passengers stopped to compliment the family on how beautiful Camille was and congratulate Zeek and Kahlani on their nuptials in Hawaii.

After 9 hours and 10 minutes on a plane the family finally landed and were greeted by James and Rosemarie. After greetings and everyone getting their Lei Zeek asked where Ramona was? Oh she's with the wedding coordinator finishing off any last minute touches for your big day son James answered. With that they dropped the girls off at the resort while all the men stayed at the house with James. Christian and Malcolm missed their little sister already so they face timed Harmony and Kahlani all day just to see Camille smile. The boys whined that these would be the longest 3 days of their lives to be away from the girls but it will be so worth it.

Ch 18: The Wedding Day

That beautiful morning sunrise was the first thing Kahlani saw after opening her eyes.It made a huge smile appear on her face so she sent a text to both Malcolm and Christian saying "I can't wait until we all have the same last name this afternoon". Within seconds the boys text her saying " I can't wait either but you've always been my mom". Then the official alarm clock sounded in the form of Camille needing a diaper change which woke everyone up. After breakfast it was time for the wedding festivities.

The men went with James to the barber and the ladies went to the spa with Ramona and Rosemarie. Then it was off to the hair salon where an older black woman approached Kahlani asking in a threatening manner " do you know Marcus Coleman young lady"? Yes, he's my father. How do you know him? Kahlani replied. I'm your grandmother Rita Coleman, he never told the family about you or your mother but when the news report of how he died came out I knew I had to find and meet you. I'm so sorry for what my son did to you all those years ago baby. I don't have much time left on earth and I'd like to spend it getting to know my granddaughter.

With a face full of tears Kahlani held Rita and said; grandma I'm getting married today would you like to spend the rest of the day with up? Ritas' face lit up as she replied I'd love to baby. Then Kahlani couldn't help but ask Rita how she found her in Hawaii, was she traveling alone or with someone else? Rita held both of her hands and told Kahlani everything from how she hired a private investigator to having one of her cousins bring her to Hawaii to see Kahlani in-person. Overwhelmed by the news Kahlani let Rita know that after today she was going to be having a second wedding back in Richfield and would love for her to be in attendance. With teary eyes Rita replied I've missed out on enough, I won't miss your wedding for anything in the world.

Now the ladies had their hair and make-up done and were headed back to the hotel to relax until time for the wedding. Rita was invited to tag along so Kahlani could catch up with the family she never knew. Most of the time Rita just stared at Kahlani in awe of the mixture of Ramona and her son sitting before her. Kahlani being the nurturer she is made sure all of her elders had something to eat before she fed herself and her daughters. By 3 pm it was time to get ready for the wedding and everyone hugged the bride dispersed except the bridal party. Ramona and Rosemarie headed for the beach while Janette took Rita to meet the groom.

At the house Zeek and his groomsmen were just about to leave when Janette walked in with an elderly woman. Ma why are you here and not at the beach or with the girls Zeek asked. Well son Ms. Rita wanted to meet the man who is going to take care of her only granddaughter Janette replied. Zeek walked over and gave Rita a hug whispering in her ear" I'll take good care of her just like she's done for me and my children". Then he turned around to introduce Rita to Malcolm and Christian who were all smiles. Finally in the car everyone was heading to the beach for the wedding. James continued to check making sure his granddaughter was keeping it together, not second guessing her choice to be with such a good man like Zeek.

Upon arrival everyone got out of the car waiting to see Camille in her little wagon ride down the aisle. At first Camille was fussy when Kahlani put her in the wagon but when she saw big sister she was all smiles then started clapping. Once she was down the aisle one look at her dad and brothers made her want to be picked up.Malcolm went over to pick her up and the whole beach was filled with admiration for the smile on that 7 month olds face. Next James appeared under the arch next to his beautiful bride leaving Zeek speechless. As they came down the aisle Zeek and Christian became emotional with tears so Kahlani stopped to wipe christians' tears. At the altar she reached up to wipe away Zeeks' as well with a smile as radiant as a sunset.

The minister called everyone to attention stating: after meeting this couple they're proof that you can find love by any means possible. Whether through trauma or tragedy no matter the circumstance you can be triumphant in the end. Just as it says in **Ps 54:7 For he saves me from every distree, And I will look in triumph on my enemies.** After all these two have endured together and apart this momentous occasion today is a triumphant way to start a future. At this time the couple would like to say their vows so at this time we'll start with the bride.

Kahlani- Hi Handsome on this day before all these witnesses I vow to be your helpmate in life. To watch you walk with GOD and lead our family and to be the cure for your pain. Since the day we met you were the security blanket I never knew I needed. Our first date was the start of the healing process for me. I never thought I'd be a mother and you gave me 4 people that call me Ma everyday. The moment you asked me to be your wife I knew my life goals would finally be fulfilled. As your wife I hereby promise to Love, Honor and Cherish every moment of our lives together in sickness and health for as long as we both shall live.

Zeek- Thank You Beautiful on this day before all these witnesses I vow to be the man, provider and protector that you need. To stand with Christ as the head of our family and lead you and our children in the way of the Lord. I never thought I'd ever meet a woman with the level of Class and Sophistication that you carry yourself with everyday. It makes my heart glad to see my children happy every morning about going to school. I'm sad that I'm not their favorite person to talk to anymore but, what can I say they needed a Mother figure. I Thank You and Love You for being the Woman you are to me and our children. As your husband I hereby promise to Love,Honor and Obey your every wish for as long as we both shall live.

After hearing those beautiful vows all that's left to say is Ezekiel Williams you may now kiss your bride the minister responded. The one thing Zeek had been waiting to hear for the last 3 days was finally spoken into existence. He planted a kiss on the lips of his wife that made her feel like she was floating on air. Then it was on to the beach party/reception outside of their hotel. The men changed into shorts and the ladies changed into party dresses. Everyone enjoyed a traditional Hawaiian meal and roasted marshmallows and laughed till the wee hours of the morning.

Ch 19: Second Wedding

After their Hawaiian Wedding the couple sent the kids home with Janette to finish the school year. Mr & Mrs Ezekiel Williams stayed 2 more weeks in Hawaii to enjoy some time away from the kids. The night before they were due to go home Zeek looked over at Kahlani and replied; Hey, my wife wanna come over here and lay on the beach with me. Kahlani turned over in the bed to see Zeek standing by the bed with his hand out in her direction. Looking down at his hand Kahlani grasped his hand and walked out to the beach to watch the sunset together.

By June 15th the couple had returned back to Richfield to have their second wedding in the Kingdom Hall. All the kids were just as excited for this ceremony as they were for the first one. One of Mrs. Johnsons' closest friends Sis. Crockett volunteered to make the food for them. Sis. Pickett offered to decorate the hall for the event of the summer for the Williams family. And Rita offered to help any way Kahlani needed her to, there was nothing this woman wouldn't do for her granddaughter.

By the 29th it was time to have their second wedding to make the bride happy again. The men were at the hall getting dressed while the ladies got dressed at Ritas'. Before leaving Kahlani just walked around looking at all the pictures of her father around the living room. At this time Camille was 8 months old and crawling all over the place her mother placed her feet. Harmony walked into the living room and picked up her little sister then followed Kahlani around the room asking who was in those pictures. Baby girl the man in these photos is my father who raped and molested me when I was little. The sound of an engine got their attention so they looked out the window to find the limo parking in front of the house.

On the ride to the hall Rita held Kahlani by the hand while watching Harmony hold a sleeping Camille in her lap. This time Malcolm walked Kahlani down the aisle for the ceremony this time around. After walking her down the aisle brother Jacobs asked: who gives this woman to be married to this man? The 3 older children said: we do and little Camille shouted"Me" making everyone laugh. Then Bro.Jacobs began with the talk saying:in **Hebrews 13:4 we are commanded to Let marriage be honorable among all, and let the marriage bed be without defilement.** Don't let any outsiders into your marriage and stop the two of you from loving one another.

The two of you have made so much progress to get to this point in your lives. Satan is always lying in wait to disrupt the joy and sanctity of marriage. You must put Jesus as the head of your marriage by making a 3 fold cord of strength. Entering into marriage you two are welcoming the words of **John 2:2** where it tells us that **Jesus and his disciples were also invited to the marriage feast.** By including Christ and all these witnesses into your celebration your marriage will be strong and will not waiver. In closing you are truly a lovely couple and Kahlani I know Sis. Johnson is proud of the decisions you've made in your adult life. After a short prayer Bro. Jacobs pronounced them man and wife telling Zeek he could now kiss his bride. After a 2 hour dinner party with everyone at the hall the Williams Family of 6 headed home for the night.

Kahlani turned to Zeek and asked him a simple question: Husband, do you know what we forgot to do? What did we forget to do, wife,Zeek inquired? We didn't choose a place to go for our honeymoon Mr. Williams. Well Mrs. Williams I told you that your wish is my command so decide all I'll show up. So if I want to go on a cruise you won't protest against it. Not at all Babygirl, Zeek answered. And if I want our honeymoon to be a couples trip with our friends,

Kahlani asked. I don't care as long as they don't bother us while we consummate our marriage, Zeek said with a smile.

Ch20: Roger's causing trouble from the inside

You'd think this family would be able to finally have peace in their lives but, as usual the devil is lying in wait. On the 4th of July Kahlani took her daughters to visit Rita but were given some unexpected news upon arrival. Her cousin Vaughn informed Kahlani that Roger had been sending threatening letters to Rita since the beginning of June. She asked to see the letters so Vaughn went to get them from the back room and handed them to Kahlani. After seeing the first letter Kahlani was terrified and called Zeek immediately with the news about Roger.

Roger was furious upon hearing the news and told his wife he was on his way there as they spoke. After hanging up Zeek called Richards and Lewis telling them what Roger was doing from the inside. When he got to Ritas' both she and Kahlani were in tears still reading more letters. Zeek walked over and took the letters out of her hands and wrapped his arms around both of them saying: Don't worry I'll take care of it. Kahlani said to him,I don't understand why your dad has this obsession with hurting me. Now he wants to use my grandma and Camille as leverage against me.

Baby did you forget you married a cop, Roger can't get past me from the inside. This ends tomorrow when I go back into the station because these letters shouldn't have made it out of the prison. Ms. Rita don't worry you'll never receive another letter from my father again after tomorrow and that's my word. You are just as important to me as my wife and children are to me and I protect those close to me. If you don't feel safe in your home you can stay with my mom next door to us.

Rita was surprised and asked: Do you really live next door to your mother? Zeek nodded his head to say Yes then explained to her the situation. The house my mother lives in was owned by my foster mother while my mom was in rehab. When my mom came home my foster mother gave us the house and moved to Florida. The house that I was abused in by my dad was condemned by the state and bulldozed to the ground. When I graduated from College I had it rebuilt for me and my kids and now my family. That story touched Rita so much that she started crying again and wrapped her arms around him.

In the meantime Roger sat in the wreck area lifting weights until one of his homeboys walked over to chat. Roger asked: what up slick what's the word on the street about my favorite girl. Slick replied: word is that she got the letters and your son isn't too happy about it. He is coming up here tomorrow to see you, you should be worried about this cause your son is really mad about your actions.Roger put the weights down and looked at Slick replying: I'm not worried about Zeek he may think he has pull in here, but he doesn't have any pull on the outside like I do.

You sure about that because he has been locking up every member of the crew in the last 3 days, Slick asked. This caught Roger's attention and made him uneasy regarding his son. Do you know when my son is coming up here to the prison? I heard the guards saying he'll be up here tomorrow to see you and he's not happy at all. He'll get over it, he shouldn't be holding onto what I did to him over 30 years ago.

Ch 21: Zeek and Roger's final showdown

The next day Zeek was at the prison right before lunch with Richards and Lewis in tow. To say Zeek was mad is an understatement, he was livid with Roger making threats on the life of his wife and 9 month old daughter. Zeek wouldn't even speak to any of his co-workers as he walked into the visitation room. While he waited for Roger to be brought down he handed Richards and Lewis a list of questions for Roger.

When Roger entered the room with a smile on his face,it quickly faded at the sight of his son having back up with him. Just as he sat down Roger sarcastically smiled at Zeek and asked: what brings you in here son and how was your holiday? Zeek didn't even blink; he just looked over to Richards and nodded his head. Richards looked down at the list and asked Roger: Why do you have an obsession with your daughter-in-law ? Roger smiled and looked directly at Zeek as he answered: so son you actually married my favorite, so you've been in that valley between her legs. Let me ask you son, is it as good as it was when she was 3? I just can't get over that and want her to give me a trip down memory lane.

Both Richards and Lewis were disgusted by Roger's answer so they turned to Zeek to see if he wanted to continue. Zeek nodded in Lewis's direction so Lewis asked: Why would you threaten to kidnap and kill your own granddaughter? Sitting stone-faced Zeek watched for Roger's answer to the question. Roger looked his son in the eye and replied: since her mother won't come in here to give me her body freely, she's at the right age for one of my associates to do what want to do to her and send me the tape. By this point both Richards and Lewis wanted to puke after listening to this man.

Richards and Lewis turned to leave the room but stopped to tell Roger that he was the most sick individual they'd ever met. Then Zeek stood from his seat still staring straight ahead and informed Roger bluntly; I am a christian when it comes to my wife and kids I will kill you for them. Roger you just charged your sentence from 99 years to the death penalty for this. Lastly; why are you threatening Marcus's mother when you helped that man rape and abuse her granddaughter. Roger leaned back in his seat to look up at his son and said: He never wanted them to meet so I was making sure she stayed away from her granddaughter like he asked.

So your loyalty is to a dead man instead of minding your own business and leaving my wife alone. I'm not going to tell you again you are to have no contact with my family at all while you're here. Roger turned up his nose and replied "Your Family" boy I'm your family not Kahlani or Rita. Zeek stopped by the door and responded to Roger saying: they are more family to me than you'll ever be. For what you did to me and Kahlani, you're dead to me and my kids. Don't underestimate me here Roger i'll kill you and everyone associated with you for my family.

It's clear Roger was giving Zeek a real headache with all his antics but little did Zeek know that Roger was just getting started. Zeek left there even madder than he was when he got there. He had to figure out how to protect his family from his own father. There was only one call he could think of making at this very moment walking out of the prison.

Ch 22: Roger's in the hot seat

Zeek called his lawyer to meet him at the courthouse to take a meeting with the judge with regards to Roger Williams. When Zeek walked into the judge's chambers with the letters in hand they greeted him and he responded with a head nod. Well OK let's get started shall we Judge Anthony stated. So Zeek, what brings you in today you did sound pretty angry on the phone his lawyer proclaimed.

I wanted answers directly from him but I knew I'd do something crazy if I went alone so I took backup with me. Then Zeek took out a tape recorder and pressed play then took a seat next to his lawyer. After 2 minutes of listening Judge Anthony asked Zeek if he had the letters with him, to which Zeek nodded and pulled them out of his pocket. Zeek handed them over to Judge Anthony and the 3 men continued to listen to the recording in silence. By the end both the lawyer and judge could feel the steam coming out of Zeek's ears from his rage.

When the tape ended Judge Anthony and the lawyer were disgusted by Roger's opinion of women and children. Then Judge Anthony spoke up asking: do we know who was on duty on the days these letters went out in the mail. Yes, Officer Latrell and Officer Mitchell were on duty on the days Zeek replied. And an informant on the inside had told Officer Richards those officers do have a sexual relationship ongoing with Roger. Judge Anthony just shook his head in disgust at the actions of these 2 female officers.

Mr. Williams thank you for bringing this information to the court's attention and I give you my word it will be handled immediately. Mr. Williams before you go I'd also like to let you know that you and your wife don't have to appear in court this time around. Your attorney will speak on your behalf if that's alright with you sir. Zeek shook hands with both of the men and headed home to his family. Upon entering his home Zeek explained everything to his wife to give her comfort and a sense of security. Later that night a knock on the door startled Zeek who was putting Camille back to bed after changing her pamper. Being an officer of the law, Zeek grabbed his service weapon and went to answer the door. On the other side of the door were 2 of his father's associates with a message for him but he had a message for Roger as well.

Before the men could finish saying the message was from Roger, Zeek shot the man to his left in the hand to disarm him of his weapon. Then he told the man to his right to give Roger a message for him in the morning. Tell Roger next time he thinks of sending someone to harm me or my family, it'll be a bullet to the head not just the hand tonight was a warning. And tell him to stop trying my patience. It's making his case worse for him, not me. With that Zeek closed the door and headed up stairs for bed but sent a text to Lewis about what just happened then called it a night.

Roger is really a piece of work and he's trying the wrong one right now. Zeek doesn't play about his woman and his kids and Roger has crossed the line in that interrogation room. So how will Roger push his luck with his son in these streets?

Ch 23: Seat on Death Row

The next morning Lewis stopped by Zeek's house to talk about the text from last night but was surprised to find a note on Zeek's car. Reading the note Lewis knocked on the door with urgency to speak to his partner. When the door opened Zeek was surprised to see his partner there so early. Hey man it's not time to start our shift yet, what brings you here so early? I'm not even dressed yet. Lewis handed the note to Zeek and said just read this man.

Zeek took the note just as Kahlani walked down the stairs holding Camille headed to the kitchen to feed her. Kahlani stopped to give Lewis a hug and asked him: what brought you here so early, adding extra security at my house. Lewis nodded his head saying: Just like your husband it's my job to serve and protect you along with my nieces and nephews. You mean until Malcolm graduates from the academy then all 3 of you guys will serve and protect me. Lewis looked over at Zeek in shock, unaware of Malcolm wanting to join Law Enforcement then turning to Kahlani to reply Yes Ma'am.

Then she was off to the kitchen to make breakfast and feed Camille before the other kids got up. Soon as the coast was clear Zeek pulled out his phone to call his lawyer about the situation at hand. His lawyer told him he was on his way to the house to pick up the note and would take it straight to the judge. After breakfast Zeek and Lewis sat outside until Zeek's lawyer pulled up to get the note. He stood by the car to read the note which said: Just give us the baby and Roger will leave you alone. He looked over at Zeek and replied: man your father really is a sick individual but go about your day as usual and I'll take care of this for your family. Then he was off to the courthouse to see Judge

Anthony about their next move with Roger.Once Judge Anthony saw the note he informed Zeek's lawyer that this case had to be moved up to next week this can't keep going on.

Judgement Day for Roger got here quickly and was swift for all to see in and outside of the courtroom. This time there wasn't a jury to decide Roger's fate, it was just Judge Anthony, the lawyers and Roger himself. When Roger was brought into the courtroom a cold chill strolled in behind him. He looked up at the Judge waiting to see what his fate would be now. Judge Anthony sat staring at Roger with fury in his eyes then spoke directly to him. Mr.Williams the last time we were here when I handed down your sentence you were told to not have any contact with your son's family.

Since you decided to defy my ruling and harass your daughter-in-law and the mother of your dead friend as well as your grandchildren. The court has seen the threats you've sent to Rita Coleman and Kahlani Williams. We also read the note your associates left at your son's home regarding kidnapping your granddaughter. Being that you are a known child predator the court hereby sentences you to spend the rest of your natural life on death row.Every person in the room gasped at the sentence Judge Anthony handed down to Roger Elias Williams. You Mr.Williams have shown that you don't like to follow the rules that are put in place for the safety of others around you. Now you will be at the mercy of others who, like yourself, pose a threat to society. There will be no sending or receiving of any mail pertaining to you or your victims on the outside. If somehow this does happen your co-conspirators will be dealt with accordingly and your execution will be happening sooner than you think the court will adjourn.

Ch 24: Another Plot

In the Women's Prison Melody and Destiny were plotting again but didn't think of what the outcome would be. Then during lunch the two were sitting alone at a table trying to figure out a plan . How are we going to get out of here to get rid of her and get our children back. The ladies had murder on their minds and Kahlani had to go fast. All of Roger's associates have been taken off the streets by Zeek so they had no help on the outside.

Melody told Destiny to simply let just finish the mission Roger gave us before we got caught. Firstly Melody stated:I saw you talking to that cute guard last night. Do you think you can get him to sneak us out of here? Destiny blushed and said: I don't know, maybe I can make something up to get out. Girl, please try I need to get out of here and get my kid back, we can share the man because we have kids with him anyway. Girl, you are so right about that now enough reminiscing about Officer Williams and let's focus on our freedom.

I hear you Mel after dinner. I'll talk to him when he gets here for the night shift and let you know. After dinner Officer Reynolds walked in for his shift and locked eyes with Destiny making all the ladies swoon. Then when everybody went to bed Destiny stayed out at the officer's station to start the plan. Hey, baby I wanted to ask you a question Destiny stated. Sure, Love you can ask me anything the officer replied giving her a sweet kiss. Well I want to see my daughter and her dad won't bring her here to see me. Do you think you could convince them to let me have an off site visitation with my daughter, I've been a model prisoner.

I know you have baby but they may not agree even with my recommendation, but I'll try for you. Now step into my office and show me how much you missed me today. I always miss you officer but I really hope you can help me see my daughter. Don't worry about it, just give me 1 week and it will be taken care of just for you. My friend is locked in this block also and wants to see her son after I come back from seeing my daughter. Can you help her out too for me?

Is she going to give me the same sweet treats you give me every night if I help her out. I'm not sure I haven't asked her about that yet, but I'll ask her after breakfast and let you know tomorrow night. Alright but until then let's do what we do every night beautiful. With that the two made love behind the guards desk with all the other prisoners peeking out of the glass panels on their cell doors. The next morning Officer Reynolds was gone and Destiny had to talk to Melody about the plan. Hey, Mel she greeted coming out of her cell to get in line for her tray. So what did he say? Will he help us get out of here or do we need to come up with another plan. Well, Mel he said he'd help me get out but if you want his help you'll have to do what I did last night as payment for his help. Are you serious? I have to sleep with the man in order to get out of here.

That's what he said Mel, the choice is yours do you want to see Malcolm or state in here for the rest of your life? It was a no brainer for Melody she salivated over the thought of being near her son and getting rid of Kahlani. So Melody looked at her tray then looked at Destiny and said: So if I do this he'll help me get closer to Malcolm. That's what he told me last night Mel so what do you say? Is Malcolm worth it or not? I know Harmony is worth it for me.

The following week it was game time for Destiny as she strategically laid out her plan in her head. She went over to Melody in the corner to share it with her all smiles. Listen, Mel after dinner I'm going to pretend to be sick so he can take me to see the nurse. On the way to the nurse I'm going to dip down the stairwell and out of the emergency exit. He has rented me a getaway car with a change of clothes to make my getaway. Once I locate the kids I'll contact him to get you all squared away for your escape. I'll pull up to get you and we're home free to live and be around our kids. Sounds good right Destiny said excitedly with all smiles. Yeah, Des that sounds great I can't wait for it to happen. Me neither girl but it's almost time so let me go get ready to do some great acting.

By 9pm Officer Reynolds was walking in for his shift and just as planned Destiny pretended to be sick. Officer Sheffield offered to take her to the nurse but Reynolds insisted he'd take Destiny before clocking in for his shift. The plan was going smoothly from that very moment. Down the hall Reynolds took the cuffs off and made sure the coast was clear before telling her to go. With one final kiss she was gone down the stairs to the outside world. How is the plan going to play out from here? Let's find out shall we.

Ch25: Escape Accomplice

Once Destiny found a place to lay low in the city she grabbed the burner phone Reynolds left in the cup holder. Sent him a text to go help Melody get out and she'll be waiting by the fire escape. While looking around the car Destiny found the stash of money he left in the center console. Destiny went into her room she rented and called Reynolds to make sure he got her text. He told her he was working on getting Melody out of the cell block and he'd call her back. Just like he did with Destiny once they got to the staircase he told Melody to run then he shot Destiny a text. **Reynolds- She's headed to the fire escape now**

Destiny- OMW I'll see you later baby

Reynolds- C U L8ter beautiful

Destiny- Luv U

Reynolds-Luv U 2

After that last text Destiny got in the car and headed back towards the prison to get Melody. Once she got to the fire escape Melody was just getting to the bottom. Destiny was trying to stay out of view of the cameras so as not to blow their cover. As soon as Melody got in the car the sirens and alarms started going off. In alarm Destiny asked Melody did this happen when she escaped? No, Reynolds intercepted the other guards before they did their rounds to see you were gone.

The ladies drove around trying to find anyone associated with Roger to help them finish their plan. When they saw every place was empty that used to be occupied by Roger and his friends they went back to the room Destiny rented. Now what can we do since everybody we used to know is off the streets thanks to Zeek. By nightfall the girls drove around the old neighborhood to see how their children were living.

Ch 26: Roger's input

After finding out that their children were living happy lives with the woman they couldn't stand. Destiny called Reynolds to ask him to go over to the men's prison and put her in touch with Roger Williams. While waiting for information from Reynolds they watched Malcolm and Harmony from a distance. On a visit with Roger, Reynolds made a call to Destiny's burner phone to let her and Melody talk to Roger.

When the call was connected destiny asked Roger for help with a place to put Kahlani to get her out of the way of their plan. Roger gave them directions to an old warehouse over the state line in NorthCarolina they could use. Destiny told Roger they'll bring Kahlani to him after they finish their mission to get their kids away from the woman they are envious of. The two were driving to the school where their children were getting out to go home. Just as they got into the pickup line and saw Kahlani standing by a car holding a little girl that looks just like Harmony.

Filled with hatred Melody said to Roger I just want to kill her right now and mail her corpse to you as a gift. Roger replied Melody , don't you ever speak about harming my sweet Kahlani. I will send someone to skin you alive if you dare to even make her bleed. Do you hear me? Roger yelled into the phone. Yeah,Yeah,Yeah we hear you Roger we got it. Don't ever harm Kahlani Destiny said dryly. Just as they were about to hang up the girls watched Zeek walk out of the school with Malcolm and Harmony. Then Zeek walked directly toward Kahlani and kissed her then kissed the toddler in her arms. Lastly; they watched both Malcolm and Harmony kiss the toddler who was smiling with her arms in the air reaching for Malcolm.

Ch 27: Life back to normal

Now with Roger out of the way everyone can live freely and enjoy their lives. Zeek and Kahlani went on more dates while Malcolm and Harmony watched their younger siblings. Keeping the romance alive Janette started going on dates as well and would call Ramona to gossip about them. The two ladies would share some great laughs about Janette's dating history. Janette is the most hilarious serial dater on earth in the mind of Ramona who calls her daughter after listening to Janette.

One night Janette told Ramona she would call her around 10 pm if the date went well. But Janette called Ramona at 8:30 telling her she ended the date early because he kept talking to his mother during dinner. Girl, he had to explain to his mother how to program her t.v. Then we went to her house on the way back and the woman was sitting in the living room wearing a bra and watching t.v. Ramona tried to hold in her laughter until Janette said she went to find the bathroom and stopped dead in her tracks when she saw an elderly man dancing by himself to Teddy Pendagrass naked. Ramona screamed in laughter at this story because Janette is known to be extra.

As usual Ramona called her daughter to pass on the gossip to her and Harmony before bed. Even during working hours Zeek would receive calls from the ladies with stories that ended with side splitting laughter. When he worked the night shift Kahlani would call him just to say she missed him and hear Camille call him dada. One night she called him just to ask him what they could possibly do with their hilarious mothers, mainly his. Zeek replied: baby i have no idea, at first I thought she would be good in the dating game but it's just a comedy show. And your mom is traumatized thanks to your dad so I don't know if she'll ever date again.

Well at least we haven't had that problem since we met. I've had such a fun time with you that I get sad everytime you leave the house. Baby don't be sad remember it's my job to protect and serve you Zeek replied and it's my job too Lewis yelled into the phone. Kahlani laughed and said: Thank You bro I appreciate you so much for that. I'm glad you do because Regina will kill me if anything happens to you, Lewis relayed. So Rashad you're the reason Regina is so cheerful every morning at work. Zeek looked over at his partner in shock while Lewis just smiled and looked out the window. Shocked, Kahlani told the fellas she had to call Regina right now to talk about this.

Kahlani called Regina who was on the phone with Cora planning a couples night for the 3 couples on Friday night. When she joined the call the first thing the ladies heard was Kahlani yelling:Regina why didn't you tell me you were dating my husband's partner? Surprised Regina asked how did you find out about us Lani? I wanted to surprise you on our group date Friday night. Well I guess I should go ahead and tell you I'm dating Max, Cora said nervously into the phone. Kahlani was having major sensory overload at this point of the call so she made a suggestion. Girls, I think we should invite my mother-in-law and her date to go with us as well. Then she went into telling them all the stories of Janette's past dates and had her friends in tears from laughter.

Ch 28: Ramona's Secret

On the big island of Hawaii Rosemarie was getting Ramona ready to go on a date for the first time in 27 years. After overcoming her PTSD Ramona was still worried about interacting with men again. The man is the same age of 55 like Ramona was a Chef at restaurant James and Rosemarie frequented. One afternoon while out shopping, Chef Jean how are you Rosemarie shouted across the parking lot? Rosemarie, do you need help with your bags? Chef Jean asked? Thank You that would be nice, Rosemarie replied.

While putting the bags in the car for her, Rosemarie asked Chef Jean if he'd go on a date with her daughter Ramona? Chef Jean agreed just so Rosemarie wouldn't send James to ask him while on their fishing trip. By the end of the week Chef Jean was on his way to pick up his date at the home of his fishing buddy. When he arrived and knocked on the door it was opened by a beautiful younger version of rosemarie. Chef Jean walked Ramona to the car, holding the door for her to get in. Then they made their way to dinner at Chef Jean's home on the beach for dinner.

After dinner and great conversation and dancing the two made their way to take Ramona home. Once they were there Ramona turned to Chef Jean and told him how much she enjoyed herself that night and hoped they could do this again. Chef Jean agreed and walked her to her door giving her a kiss on the cheek. Once she was safely in the house chef Jean made his way back to his car and back to his home. The next day at breakfast James and Rosemarie Asked about her date with Chef Jean? Blushing Ramona said it was the best date ever. So when are you going to see him again Rosemarie asked excitedly?

Relax Rose let her enjoy getting to know the man, you're practically pushing her to the altar after 1 date, James exclaimed. After cleaning up Ramona goes outside to call Janette and tell her about her date. From the kitchen window Rosemarie could see her daughter all smiles thinking she was talking to Chef Jean she clapped with joy. James look look she's on the phone with him and she's smiling with joy. It's Only 1 date and Rosemarie is being just as extra as Janette.

Ramona begged Janette not to tell Kahlani about this right now. Ramona wants to tell her daughter about her new relationship with a Chef personally.That's without Janette's extra details to make it sound as hilarious as her dating life.

Ch 29: Jailbird comes home

The ladies thought that being entertained by Janette was a great idea for their date night and couldn't wait for a good laugh. They didn't even tell the men about this addition to the plan to surprise them the whole night. When Friday came and Cora kept telling Kahlani all day how she couldn't wait for the day to be over so their date night could start. When they got home Kahlani and Zeek fed the kids and made sure the younger kids were bathed and in bed before leaving. Zeek told Malcolm and Harmony to call them if anything goes wrong, little did he know trouble was on the way.

All four couples met up at the bowling alley for the first part of their date night. After 3 fun battle of the sexes games it was time for dinner. Unbeknownst to them on the way to dinner Destiny had somehow escaped from the Women's Prison. While making an excuse of needing to see the nurse Destiny kicked the guard in the stomach and made a quick dash out of a side door. Nobody knows how she got out of those cuffs and hitchhiked her way back to Richfield. During dinner Janette started to interview her date about his relationship with his mother. All her questions had the whole restaurant laughing uncontrollably so everybody got takeout containers for their food.

After 45 minutes of laughter Kahlani excused herself from the table to use the bathroom. Once she was done on her way back to the table her cell rang with a call from Harmony so she stepped back into the bathroom to answer it. Hey baby girl, how's everything at the house? Harmony hysterically yelled: she took them, she took them Ma. Harmony slow down for me. Christian and Camille were taken by my mom, she broke in and hit Malcolm in the head then ran up the stairs which woke me up. Ok calm down and call for an ambulance for Malcolm we'll take care of the rest.

Overwhelmed with grief, Kahlani ran back to the table to get the boys to help. Kahlani ran to the table yelling Rashad, Max, Zeek you need to go find my babies now. What are talking about how do you know something is wrong with the kids? Harmony called while I was in the bathroom, she said Destiny had escaped and showed up at the house. She broke in and knocked out Malcolm in the living room while he was sleeping on the couch.Then she went upstairs to Camille's room and came out holding her and went into Christians room and she could hear him struggling to breath. She hid behind the door to her room and watched Destiny drag Christian down the stairs and out the door.

By the time she got down stairs she could see the tail lights of a red chevy trailblazer leaving the driveway.

Rashad asked did she get the plate number Lani so we could track it. Umm she said it was LTB4251 now go get my babies I'm going to the hospital to check on Malcolm. All the men left together in one car after paying for the meal while Regina drove all the ladies to the hospital.Upon entering the hospital Kahlani demanded to know where her children were in that building. The nurse at the desk took the ladies up to the 5th floor where Harmony was sitting in tears. Janette Wrapped her arms around Harmony while Kahlani begged every doctor and nurse on that floor to give her information on her son. During this time the men were on their phones with dispatch and other officers to track down Destiny and the kids.

Kahlani told Cora and Regina to head home and she'd call them when she had more information. After they left Kahlani sat down next to Harmony and held hands in anticipation. Then the doctor came out of the room and said: Mrs. Williams Malcolm will be fine, it's just a mild concussion he'll wake up in a couple of hours. Thank You Doc. Samson Kahlani replied. Then he was gone and she was left with Harmony holding Malcolms' hands just waiting. By 11am Malcolm finally opened his eyes to see his sister and step-mom at his side with teary eyes. The first thing he asked was where his siblings found and all the tears came back to Kahlani and Harmony. Dad is out there with uncle Rashad and uncle Max searching for them Harmony answered. Malcolm also let tears fall from his eyes and started blaming himself for the situation. No brother don't blame yourself you didn't know my mom would escape prison and come to our house. One day you're going to be just like your dad and save all of our lives just like he is right now.

To liven the mood Harmony said: Bro when you get out of here we'll find you a girlfriend. As if in cue Malcolm said: Ew sis that's not gonna happen for me maybe for Christian. Kahlani couldn't help but laugh at her children as she waited for word of the safety of her other 2 children. Then Kahlani turned to Malcolm and Harmony and asked: how about a little story time about your grandma's dating life? They looked at each other and said in unison "Sure".

Ch 30: SerialDaterStories(Kahlani speaking)

Let's take into account that Janette is 58 and hasn't been on a date since meeting Roger in 1981. So the dating world of 2019 is hard for her to understand and men are very different nowadays. I knew Janette was traumatized by her relationship with Roger but it's starting to show in her taste in men. When I was planning the weddings I kept telling her she should start dating again and bring her date to the weddings. But she chose to wait until after the weddings to start dating on Tinder.

Date(1) Janettee matched with a lawyer who lived in Cattle Ranch Village. He came to pick her up in this brand new 2020 Buick Enclave so far so good. He takes her to an expensive Italian Restaurant where his mother is waiting for them at the table. They talk while waiting for their drinks and after placing their meal orders. When the food arrived he took her plate and cut up all the chicken on her plate for her and sat it in front of her. Then his mother doesn't touch her food but takes a piece of chicken off Janettte's plate to eat. Then she takes her son's plate to cut up his steak and feed it to him. So Janette, being her extra self, stood up and announced to everyone " this is why you're single and can't get a real woman because you're in a consensual relationship with your mother". She ordered 3 extra meals to go and charged it to his black card before she got an Uber to go home.

Date(2) She decided to try tinder again and matched with a Doctor at a hospital across town. He took her bowling which was cool and all but when he spent more time at the counter than with her it became a problem. Janette stood behind him to eavesdrop on the conversation for 10 minutes. Turns out the lady at the counter was his wife and they were planning their 5th wedding anniversary the whole time he was at the counter. He forgot that his credit card was next to Janette's Purse so she picked it up, ordered her Uber and went home. Then she ordered DoorDash and maxed out his card on a brand new wardrobe.

Date(3) she decided this time she'd try Bumble dating site this time and met an optometrist(eye doctor). He took her to the movies to see The Informer but just as they were about to enter the theater, a woman behind the snack counter called his name. They turned around to walk back over when the woman brought 2 kids from the back office. The kids started yelling "Daddy" running straight toward him with their arms in the air. So needless to say they watched Captain Marvel with his kids instead. Then as they left his baby mama said to us" this is how I can get you to see your kids by hacking your phone and setting you up on dates with other women at my job". Then she tells us to drop the kids off at her mother's on the way home. When he got to your grandma's house she turned to him as she got out the car and said: How are you an eye doctor but you don't even see your own kids everyday?

Date(4) The last date she went on before tonight was unreal to say the least. The man was a retired Marine working security at the mall. He took her to a seafood restaurant knowing he himself was allergic to shellfish. Your grandma knew so she told the waiter to put the shellfish on a separate plate from his side items. After having good food and conversation it was time to go home. On the way to drop your grandma off the guy got the bubble guts and started passing gas, then said: do mind if we make a stop by my place I need to change my pants?

So they go to his house and as he gets out the car a trail of brown is running down his khakis in the back. He was in such a hurry he left the car keys in the cup holder which she picked up and followed him into the house. As she enters the house the guy's mom is standing by the bathroom and gives your grandma a choice to make. Either she can sit and wait in the living room or she could wash his poop stained clothes while momma gives him a bath. Your grandma took the man's car and drove home, when he called her the next day, she told him his momma could bring him to pick it up because wasn't going to bring it to him.

Sample of book 3

After that hearty laugh both Harmony and Malcolm looked at Kahlani's solemn face and said let's pray Ma. The sound of those words made Kahlani's heart swell with pride of being their mother. The three joined hands as Harmony led them in prayer for her missing siblings.

Dear God, we ask you ro put a protective covering around our little brother and my mini me? We need them back with us, Malcolm and I feel bad enough for not protecting them and Ma is having a nervous breakdown over here. Help our dad and uncles find and bring them back by the time we can take Malcolm home. Please send our grandma a good man so she can stop going on such hilarious dates every month? And help grandma Ramona to have better taste in men than grandma Janette. Lastly, can you convince mom and dad to have another baby to expand our family Amen.In unison Kahlani and Malcolm said"Amen" that was a great prayer and we did need it.

We'll pick up from this point in book 3:
Turning a new Leaf

I enjoyed sharing these first 2 books with
you guys and can't wait to give you the
next book . See you then, Love guys

Your truly,K.Moore

Discussion Questions for Book 3

Will Roger try to escape from Death Row

Will Zeek, Max and Rashad find the kids before the night's over

Should Melody and Destiny be sent to Death Row like Roger

Will Janette continue to be a serial dater or will she settle down

Will Ramona and Chef Jean still be together in the next book

Will Kahlani meet anymore of her father's family

Will Zeek and Kahlani have another child

Will Melody want revenge for Destiny hurting her son

Will Malcolm and Harmony find Love

Will Christian and Camille be found dead or alive

Leave your answers to these questions in my inbox on: <u>tiktok.com/Leavingtraumabehind4</u>[1] <u>instagram.com/</u>[2]author_k.moore <u>facebook.com/</u>[3]Leavingtraumabehind x.<u>com/LeavingTrauma4</u>[4] email: relatablefictionwriting@gmail.com

Purchase a copy at

Walmart

IngramSpark

Barnes & Noble

Smashwords

Amazon

Draft2Digital

Apple

---

1.   http://tiktok.com/Leavingtraumabehind4

2.   http://instagram.com/soultavern_owner2020

3.   http://facebook.com/nakeialdavis-moore

4.   http://twitter.com/LeavingTrauma4

Don't miss out!

Visit the website below and you can sign up to receive emails whenever K.Moore publishes a new book. There's no charge and no obligation.

https://books2read.com/r/B-A-DOREB-CMEAD

BOOKS 2 READ

Connecting independent readers to independent writers.

About the Author

Single mother from NJ now residing in NC, I've spent over 20 yrs in customer service/management. I started writing this series in 2023 during my break at work. My love for writing started in high school writing poetry. After graduation I just wasn't feeling inspired by anything or anyone. That is until I started paying close attention to the people I interact with everyday. the conversations I have with my customers set the tone for my brand **relatable fiction writing.**As well as spearheaded the story line of each one of my series that I have and are currently writing.

Read more at urbanfictionwriting.com.